Mr. Brown Can MOO!

Can You?

By
Dr.Seuss

HarperCollins *Children's Books*

Trademark of Random House Inc.
Authorised user HarperCollins*Publishers* Ltd

The Cat in the Hat
™ & © Dr. Seuss Enterprises, L.P. 1957
All Rights Reserved

© 1961, 1989 by Dr. Seuss Enterprises, L.P.
All Rights Reserved
A Beginner Book published by arrangement with
Random House Inc., New York, USA
First published in the UK 1963
This edition published in the UK 2010 by
HarperCollins*Children's Books*,
a division of HarperCollins*Publishers* Ltd
77-85 Fulham Palace Road
London W6 8JB

Visit our website at:
www.harpercollins.co.uk

Printed and bound in Thailand

Oh, the wonderful things
Mr. Brown can do!
He can go like a cow.
He can go MOO MOO
Mr. Brown can do it.
How about you?

He can go like a bee.

Mr. Brown can

How about you?
Can you go

BUZZ
BUZZ

He can go
like a cork . . .

POP POP
POP POP

He can go like horse feet

KLOPP
KLOPP
KLOPP

He can go

EEK
EEK

like a squeaky shoe.

He can go
like a rooster . . .

COCK A
DOODLE
DOO

He can go
like an owl . . .

HOO HOO
HOO HOO

EEK EEK
EEK EEK
COCK-A-DOODLE-DOO
HOO HOO   HOO HOO

How about you?

He can go like a train

CHOO CHOO
CHOO
CHOO

Oh, the wonderful things
Mr. Brown can do!

Moo Moo
Buzz Buzz
Pop Pop Pop
Eek Eek
Hoo Hoo
Klopp Klopp Klopp
Dibble Dibble
Dopp Dopp
Cock-a-Doodle-Doo

Mr. Brown can do it.
How about you?

. . . like the soft,
soft whisper
of a butterfly.

Maybe YOU can, too.
I think you ought to try.

He can go
like a horn. . .

BLURP
BLURP
BLURP
BLURP

. . . like a big cat drinking

He can go like a clock.
He can

TICK

He can

TOCK

He can go
like a hand
on a door . . .

KNOCK
KNOCK

TICK TOCK
TICK TOCK
KNOCK KNOCK
KNOCK

Oh, the wonderful things
Mr. Brown can do!

BLURP BLURP
SLURP SLURP

COCK-A-DOODLE-DOO

KNOCK KNOCK KNOCK

and HOO HOO HOO

He can even

SIZZLE
SIZZLE

He can do that, too,
like an egg
in a frying pan.
How about you?

Mr. Brown is smart,
as smart as they come!
He can do
a hippopotamus
chewing gum!

GRUM
GRUM
GRUM
GRUM
GRUM
GRUM
GRUM

Mr. Brown is
so smart
he can even do this:
he can even
make a noise
like a goldfish kiss!

BOOM BOOM BOOM

Mr. Brown is a wonder!

BOOM BOOM BOOM

Mr. Brown makes thunder!

He makes lightning!

SPLATT SPLATT SPLATT

And it's very, very hard
to make a noise like that.

Oh, the wonderful things
Mr. Brown can do!

Moo Moo
Buzz Buzz
Pop Pop Pop

Eek Eek
Hoo Hoo
Klopp Klopp Klopp

Dibble Dibble
Dopp Dopp
Cock-a-Doodle-Doo

Grum Grum
Grum Grum
Choo Choo Choo

Boom Boom
Splatt Splatt
Tick Tick Tock

Sizzle Sizzle
Blurp Blurp
Knock Knock Knock

A Slurp and a Whisper
and a Fish Kiss, too.

Mr. Brown can do it.
How about YOU?